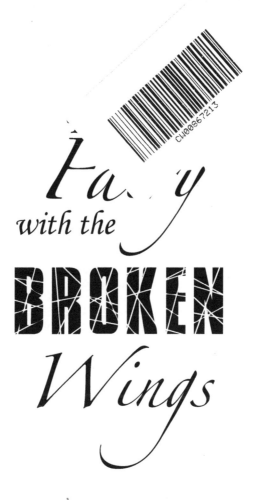

Fairy
with the
BROKEN
Wings

Will Wood

Grosvenor House
Publishing Limited

The right of WillWood to be identified as the author of this
work has been asserted in accordance with Section 78
of the Copyright, Designs and Patents Act 1988

The book cover picture is copyright to WillWood

This book is published by
Grosvenor House Publishing Ltd
Link House
140 The Broadway, Tolworth, Surrey, KT6 7HT.
www.grosvenorhousepublishing.co.uk

This book is a work of fiction. Any resemblance to
people or events, past or present, is purely coincidental.

A CIP record for this book
is available from the British Library

ISBN 978-1-78623-248-9

As we venture through this journey we call life, one tends to look at others who in some shape or form, inspire us to reach our goals and to fulfil our dreams. Great women or men that are an example for us to follow. The norm is to look at those older than ourselves in wonder and amazement, that one day we will be like them. But when the norm reaches out and provides other options one can't avoid the feeling of total bewilderment.

Many of the phrases in this book and attitudes of the main character are a never-ending example of the joy, determination and resourcefulness she expresses every day of her life. Hence, inspired by her unconditional love and trust, this book is dedicated to my granddaughter Victoria.

Sometimes, children just need a little bit of space. Space where they can hide from the anxieties and suffering of the real world, from injustice, cruelty, abuse, war and fear. It's a place just to be alone; a quiet place of their own, sometimes even to get away from the grown-ups who are always on at them to do this and that! In this place, even if just for a few moments, their imagination can set them free.

This is a story about a child who, like any other child in the world, just needed a little space. This is a story about Esperanza, a little girl who, even in the midst of a terrible conflict, used her imagination to escape...

Esperanza was in her hiding place. She was on the verge of tears and was still trying to catch her breath. She could hardly recall what had happened to her or who was to blame, it didn't matter now, she was here and she felt safe. She would close her eyes, calm down and let her imagination take her away, somewhere, anywhere. Anywhere but here...

... she found herself in a boat gently moving with the waves in the middle of the ocean, with no land in sight. The sea stretched out ahead of her like a plain blue canvas on which she could create her very own world. Her imagination started to take over...

... now she found herself in a forest. Tall pine trees, with their wonderful scent, were all around her and she could feel the pine needles crunching beneath her feet as she started to move. As she walked she gradually became aware of a sound in the distance and, as she continued towards it, she realised it was the sound of someone crying. It wasn't angry or fearful crying but soft and gentle, the tears of someone who doesn't want to be overheard. Treading gently, she continued to follow the sound and to her surprise, there in a clearing, was a fairy, sitting on top of a mushroom. The fairy saw Esperanza approaching and looked at her

'Are you all right?' asked Esperanza gently. 'Are you hurt? Why are you crying?'

'I have broken my wings,' replied the fairy, 'and I can't fly home'.

'Please don't cry,' replied Esperanza, 'I'll help you. Do you know what you need to fix them?'

'It won't be easy,' said the fairy, 'We'll need to gather lots of special things together'.

Esperanza, eager to help, asked the fairy what she needed to do.

'Please sit down, said the fairy, 'I'll tell you what we need to find. My name is Moonlight by the way, what's yours?'

'I'm Esperanza', replied Esperanza, 'and I'm very happy to meet you'.

The Quest

If you want to help me Esperanza, first you must collect three different types of dust: Gold dust, Sawdust and Diamond dust. The three dusts combined with a beam of moonlight is what is needed to repair my wings. You will have to collect the dusts separately in these,' said the fairy as she handed Esperanza three little glass jars.

'Don't mix the dusts until you return here. When you find me, lay me down on the mush-room that you have covered with sawdust and spread my wings open. This must be done on the night of the full moon, which is three nights from now. Then and only then, mix the gold and diamond dust together and sprinkle it onto my wings. When the moonlight shines on them, the dust will do its magic and my wings will be repaired.'

'You will have to leave the forest and cross the Blue River, to the place where you will find the gold dust. Then you will have to enter the Whistle-blowing woods, that is where you will collect the sawdust. Go all the way through the woods and at the other side you will have arrived at the Crystal Mountain. There you must find Glitter, an alicorn that will help you secure the diamond dust. Once you have collected all three, you must hurry and return here as quickly as possible. I will be laying beneath this mushroom, as by then I will have lost most of my strength, you must cover the mushroom with the sawdust and when the moon is high in the sky and it is at its brightest, pick me up – do not worry, you will not hurt me – and lay me on the sawdust."

'Take these magic stones, which I have made into a necklace. Each stone is a different colour and each has its own strength. Blue, is for sight; purple is for courage, red, is for speed; green is for hope – like your name – and white, is to make yourself bigger or smaller.'

"You'll also need this bag. Everything that you need is inside, keep the jars in the bag to protect them. You can speak to me whenever you need to, all you have to do is whisper, I will hear you and whisper to you in return. I wish you well, please be careful. Now I must rest.'

Esperanza, who was slightly overwhelmed and quite confused, began to walk about. She wanted to get away from it all, but before she knew it, she was already making her way through the forest. Her attention skipped between the smell of the pine trees and the rustling of the leaves under her feet. The rustling was getting stronger; something was following her. She turned around quickly but could not see a thing. She started to walk again, each step a little quicker than the last.

'Moonlight, can you hear me? I think I am being followed.'

'Run, Esperanza. Run!'

Esperanza started to run as fast as her legs could take her, the rustle of leaves grew louder and suddenly she heard the howling of wolves; they were following her and preparing to attack. The howling wolves were getting closer by the second.

Esperanza clutched her bag closer and ran faster and faster. She could feel her heart beating in her chest like a frantic war drum. Breathing heavily and with aching legs, she felt that her pursuers would pounce on her at any moment. Holding the necklace close to her chest with her right hand she squeezed the green stone between her fingers, hoping to escape. As the wolves were about to catch her, the ground beneath her feet disappeared and Esperanza fell down into a hole. Landing on soft earth, she looked around trying to get her bearings while struggling to catch her breath. She was in some kind of a burrow, totally bedazzled by hundreds of tiny lights glimmering in front of her.

THE UNDERGROUND

'Welcome to the underground Esperanza, we have been waiting for you. My name is Top Mole, but you can call me Top.'

'Where am I? How did I end up here?' asked Esperanza.

'This is the underground,' replied the Mole. 'Soon I will take you to Moleburgh our capital city. You were being chased by wolves and you fell into our burrow, so now you are here.'

'How do you know my name?' asked Esperanza.

'Let's just say a little fairy told me,' replied the mole.

'You spoke with moonlight? What did she say? Is she all right?'

'She whispered to me and told me you were coming. She has asked me to guide you to the Blue River and that is what I am going to do. But first you will have to change your size, unless you want to crawl all the way.'

Esperanza held the white stone in her hand and whispered, 'I need to be the size of a mole.' Straight away she began to shrink down in size.

'This should fit you now,' muttered Top as he handed her a helmet. 'Switch on the light and follow me.'

They began to walk, making their way through a maze of tunnels. There were Moles bustling around everywhere, some coming, others going and all with the lights of their little helmets on. Esperanza saw tunnels going off in all directions. Some going up while others were coming down, but the four main arteries of the underground went straight in the direction of each of the compass points, north, south, east and west, these four were the busiest. Esperanza and Mr Top were on the main route heading north.

'Why can't we go straight to the river Mr Top, instead of wasting time in these tunnels?'

'But my dear, we are going straight to the river. In order to get there, we have to go through Moleburgh. There you will meet others that will help you. I know you are in a hurry and concerned about Moonlight, we all are, we all love Moonlight and we will do all that we can to help her restore her wings. This is the quickest route, the underground dwellers, never ever waste time.'

Esperanza heard Moonlight's whispers. *'Follow the mole. He is a good, grumpy old friend, and he will take you where you need to go.'*

Esperanza sighed and with a little reluctance agreed to follow the mole.

Moleburgh was vast and beautiful. It had everything a city needed. Large avenues and busy streets, bright tall buildings, cafés, shops and a lot of citizens, all of them moles. For an underground city, it was remarkably well lit, so much that they no longer needed their head torches. As they walked into a busy avenue, Esperanza had a secret little stretch, it was good to finally get out of the tunnels and into an open space.

Everyone was friendly, they all spoke to her as they passed by. *Hello Esperanza. Good day Esperanza. Good luck Esperanza.* Esperanza was totally enchanted by the city and its residents. She asked Top where they were heading.

'We are off to the Mall, the main shopping centre to meet up with the one who will take you to the Blue River. Be patient my dear and you will see.'

Esperanza decided to trust her guide and began to relax and enjoy the surroundings. As she glanced left and right, she saw many shops that drew her attention. She would pause on every other street corner to take it all in, she could easily spend her pocket money in such a place. For the first time since the beginning of her quest, she felt totally at ease.

The Mall was located on the north side of Plaza Main, and it was right in the heart of the city. The merchants were dismantling the stalls of what had been a very busy street market. At the centre of the square, there were stands that had been erected on three sides of the plaza.

A large elevated stage completed the enclosure. There was a concert on that night and the audience was already gathering.

'What is going on?' asked Esperanza, as they made their way through to the mall.

'Young moles love concerts and we have one on the last Friday of every month. There is one tonight.'

They finally arrived at a small café and sat at a table. A waiter appeared seemingly out of nowhere, took their order and disappeared just as quickly. Top ordered a *mole-wine* for himself and a *mole-shake* for Esperanza.

The waiter brought the drinks on a tray which he placed on the table. Esperanza noticed something else next to the drinks. Two large tickets with *VIP* written on them.

Top saw a look of despair growing on Esperanza's face. 'Don't worry, everything is fine. Just wait and you will see. The one who will take you to the Blue River will be attending the concert and you will meet him there.' The old mole drank his wine.

Esperanza and Top were seated in the front row, right in the middle; the best seats in the house. The stands were packed, and the hustle and bustle of the audience grew louder and louder. Esperanza could see the posters of the performing artist, 'He's a beaver!'

'Yes,' replied Top. 'His name is Justin.'

Esperanza giggled. 'Justin Beaver. How come there is a beaver among the moles?' she asked.

'Many years ago there was a dreadful deluge,' explained the old mole. 'The river was about to burst its banks, and if that had happened Moleburgh would have been flooded and destroyed, we wouldn't be here right now. We sent a messenger to the beavers and asked if they could build a dam to prevent the flooding. Justin's great-grandfather ordered the construction of the dam and the beavers and moles have been good friends and allies ever since.'

The concert began. Esperanza sat quietly through it all; in spite of the cheers and enthusiasm of the crowd she had a lot of things on her mind and singing along with a beaver was not one of them. The show finished in just over an hour, though to her it felt like it had lasted a lifetime. Once the concert finished and the moles started to leave the arena Top took Esperanza backstage to meet the performer.

The three of them left Moleburgh after the show taking the north tunnel towards the river, it took them about half an hour to reach their destination. They needed to get to the other bank of the river as soon as possible to collect the gold dust. The tunnel was busy with travellers entering the city. Very few were going in the opposite direction, the further along the tunnel they went the fewer travellers they encountered. At some point it appeared that they were on their own. They were side-tracked a few times due to tunnel repairs but were quickly able to get back on their route. At the end of the path, the road was split in two. A path headed east and one headed west.

'Go west, la, la, la, la, la, go west,' sang the beaver. The three of them took the path to the west.

Esperanza could feel that that they had begun walking uphill and could finally see what looked like a way out of the tunnel. Just before they left the underground, Top embraced Esperanza and wished her well.

'I leave you in good hands, I hope I will see you on the way back.' The mole then disappeared back down the path they had just travelled along. Out in the open Esperanza was quick to fill her lungs with fresh air. She didn't feel claustrophobic in the tunnels, but she is more of an outdoor being and was glad to leave the tunnels behind her.

THE
GOLD-RUSHERS

'Wow,' exclaimed Justin, as Esperanza returned to her normal size. The beaver barely made it up to her waist. She laughed.

'What's so funny?' he asked.

'You are such a cute little one,' she answered. 'Now what?'

'We will go up stream and spend the night at my parents' house. Tomorrow we will meet at the council of the gold-rushers and ask them where the best place to find the gold is.'

The terrain was flat and covered with lush vegetation. It was a cool but not cold evening; her sweater was wrapped around her waist. Esperanza often put her hand into her bag, most of the time to make sure that the jars were still ok and occasionally to search for a snack, an apple or a banana. As the evening grew darker, she could see tiny lights in the distance, they look like hundreds of static fire-flies, sticking to the black sky. She asked Justin if that was where they were heading.

'Yes, that is where I live. We will stay there tonight.'

*

After a long and tiring walk, they arrived at the front door of a little cabin.

'If you want to sleep inside, you will have to make yourself small again.'

Esperanza knew how to do that now, and holding on to her necklace once more, she began to shrink. Inside they were greeted by Justin's parents. Esperanza sat at a dining table next to his mother, Martha, who shared her concern for Moonlight.

Soon after they had eaten, Martha took Esperanza to the little room where she would spend the night. It was small and cosy with its own bathroom. In the chest of drawers adjacent to the bed was all that she might require. Fresh linen, towels and soap. Martha told her that it was once her daughter's room, but she had moved out and was now working and living in her own place, on the other side of town.

'Sweet dreams,' said Martha and kissed her goodnight.

Once she was left alone, Esperanza tucked herself into the bed and closed her eyes. The bed was warm and comfortable, she felt so snug, like a caterpillar in its cocoon, she could lay there forever.

'How are you? I will return as fast as I can, I hope...' Esperanza whispered softly hoping Moonlight would hear her.

'I know you will.'

'I'm spending the night at Justin's house and tomorrow we will go in search of the gold dust.'

'I bid you well and I'm sure you'll find the gold dust in due time. Right now, it's time to settle down for the night and regain your strength. Tomorrow will bring its own trials and demands, but for now you must rest.'

'Goodnight, Moonlight.'

'Goodnight, Esperanza. Take care.'

The next morning, they woke up early and after a succulent breakfast prepared by Martha, Esperanza thanked her hostess, who replied with a hug and a tender, 'mi casa es tu casa.'

Esperanza and Justin then left to meet the gold-rushers at the council meeting.

The council of beavers was sitting around a big pine table, there were twelve of them, six males and six females, of all ages between thirty and eighty. They showed Esperanza to her seat, at the top of the table, on a chair with an inscription that read *special guest*. They all knew why she was there and argued amongst themselves over which would be the best place to find the gold, even though none of them had been successful in this endeavour for a long time.

'Silence!' demanded Jill, the oldest of them all. 'Silence, one and all! You are just confusing the girl.'

Jill then looked at Esperanza. 'The best way to find gold, is to help someone in distress,' she said gently. 'Follow the river upstream until you find someone who needs your help.' And with that advice Jill adjourned the meeting and wished her well.

Esperanza, even more confused than when she arrived, looked at Justin.

'What's going on?' she said. 'How can someone in distress help me find gold? I don't understand.'

Don't worry, it will work out, you will see,' replied the beaver.

*

'Moonlight, Moonlight, can you hear me?' she whispered while holding the green stone between her fingers. 'Can you believe what the gold-rushers just told me?'

The gold-rushers do not find much gold because they don't really need it, but they know that gold is there and that you will find it. Do not lose hope.'

Esperanza followed Justin upstream desperately searching for something or someone in distress. She saw a beaver sitting on a fallen tree trunk.

'Excuse me sir,' she asked politely, 'are you in distress?'

'No, my dear, I'm not. I'm just having a wee rest.'

She then encountered a squirrel, that seemed to be collecting all the acorns it could find. She asked the same question.

'No,' answered the squirrel. 'I am just collecting nuts.'

Another beaver answered that she was having lunch.

'This is insane!' exclaimed Esperanza.

All of a sudden, a frantic splashing at the riverbank caught her attention. She ran over to find a salmon with its tail caught in a piece of a broken net.

'This is the one,' she thought to herself as she lifted the fish carefully out of the water, and with gentle and precise work, she untangled the fish and carefully placed it back into the river.

'Thank you, Esperanza,' said the salmon as she released it in to the water. 'Follow me.'

Justin and Esperanza ran upriver following the salmon, who would frequently leap out of the water so they could see where it was heading.

'Wait! Please wait!' shouted Esperanza. 'We can't go any further.'

She dropped down to her knees next to the side of the river watching the salmon leaping away ahead and out of reach.

She turned around and looked at Justin in the hope that he would reveal something to ease her anxiety. His face wore the same expression of apprehension as hers.

'I thought he was in distress. Did I get it all wrong?'

'I honestly don't know, I also thought it was the one,' replied Justin.

She could still see the salmon leaping in the distance and realised the fish was now making its way back. When it got closer, she saw that it was carrying a gold nugget in its mouth. Esperanza kicked her shoes off and pulled off her socks before wading into the river, where she placed her hands together as if she were noodling and a golden nugget was gently placed into her palm. Both Esperanza and the fish expressed their gratitude before going on their separate ways; the salmon upstream and Esperanza and Justin back to the village.

The gold-rushers could not believe the size of the nugget they had found, it was the biggest they had ever seen. Esperanza was not as enthusiastic, she needed the dust, not a nugget. Jill once again told everyone to calm down and asked Esperanza where she would carry the dust. Esperanza pulled one of the little jars from her bag and handed it over. Jill took both the jar and the nugget to the grinder. After a few minutes she returned with the jar full of gold dust and asked Esperanza what she wanted to do with the remains of the nugget, which was almost the same size as when she left.

'You may keep it,' she answered, 'I have what I need, thank you all very much'.

Jill explained that Justin would guide her across the river to the entrance of the Whistle-blowing woods and wished her well. They embraced and bid each other farewell. Justin and Esperanza were on their way once more.

Justin told her that they would have to go through a tunnel under the river, as someone, for no reason whatsoever, had built a wall on the other bank. They quickly found the entrance and were making their way through the tunnel, which was built by the beavers as an escape route. When they emerged on the other side of the river they found the entrance to the woods.

'I have to leave you now; once in the woods look out for the twin squirrels. They will help you. Remember "mi casa es tu casa". I wish you well, till we meet again, goodbye and good luck.'

'Thank you, so much, Justin.'

They embraced, and he was gone.

WHISTLE-
BLOWING WOODS

Esperanza was on her own. 'Moonlight, Moonlight', she whispered, 'I'm at the entrance of the woods, I have the gold dust and I'm on my way to collect the sawdust. Are you well?'

'I'm fine. Please be careful.'

Esperanza entered the woods.

Although It was midday, the woods were really dark, the trees were tall and quite close together, so only a few rays of sunlight got through the thick foliage. The ground was covered in leaves, twigs, branches and fallen trees, with tiny groups of mushrooms scattered at random, all blending into a natural carpet that decorated the earth. Esperanza was back to her normal size and was walking steadily but carefully along a path that seemed to have been trodden on by many before. She was not quite sure where she was going but hoped she would work it out as she penetrated deeper and deeper among the trees. Everything appeared to be normal, calm and silent, as you would expect in the woods, but this was too calm and too silent, something was not quite right. She caught sight of two red squirrels, with the bushiest tails she had ever seen, chasing each other up and down the trees. They appeared on her right, then on her left and suddenly they were standing right in front of her.

'Hello Esperanza, we are Rose and Mary and we are here to help you.'

'How?' asked Esperanza.

'Wait and you will see,' they replied and started their way up another tree.

Esperanza continued on the path she had chosen and could see Rose and Mary playing ahead of her, crossing from one side to the other.

'Stop!' shouted Esperanza. 'Where are we going?'

Both squirrels were standing right in front of her again.

'We have to take you to the Lumberjacks' cabins, they will help you get the sawdust that you need. But it's still a long way, follow us and we will take you there. Then we will lead you to the Crystal Mountain.'

The squirrels rushed off once more.

'Excuse me,' cried Esperanza. The squirrels landed right in front of her again. 'Could you slow down just a little?'

'We can't, we are hyperactive. Bye!'

And they were away once more. Esperanza had no choice but to let them be and try to keep up.

After walking for a few hours, keeping an eye on the squirrels and dipping in to her bag to make sure the jars were safe, she heard it: the whistling. It began quite softly and pleasant. But then it grew louder and more irritating. The noise became so loud and intense that she lost her concentration, her bearings and almost her senses. She put her hands over her ears, in an effort to shut out the racket but to no avail, she just could not block it out. She desperately called for the sisters, who reappeared in front of her immediately.

'What is this whistling? Please make it stop!'
'Keep walking Esperanza,' they advised.

The squirrels then climbed up Esperanza's legs all the way to her shoulders, wrapped themselves around her head and covered her ears with their bushy tails. The noise instantly disappeared. She did not feel at ease and wanted to leave this place as quickly as possible. She was able to concentrate now that the sound had subsided and was focusing on where she was and where she had to go. Holding the blue stone of her necklace she could clearly see the cabins far ahead in the distance, then she tightly held the red stone and ran. It did not take her long to reach an opening, which lead her to a small village. A semicircle of wooden cabins enclosed a small plaza, which had what seemed to be a council hall in its mist. Esperanza was surrounded by a handful of lumberjacks, who greeted her enthusiastically. Rose and Mary were still on her shoulders.

'This is Esperanza,' they said. 'She is here to help Moonlight.'

'We know who she is and the purpose of her visit,' said Bob as he turned his attention to the girl. 'Welcome to our village.'

They invited her into one of the cabins and sat around an open fire. Rose and Mary stayed outside and quickly made their way up one of the trees. They knew she was in good hands.

The lumberjacks were friendly people and Esperanza liked them very much. Neither tall nor small, Esperanza thought that they were just the right size. She did not have to look up or down on any of them, which she found quite amusing and comfortable. In the cabin, they expressed their concern for Moonlight and told Esperanza that they would take her into the forest at daybreak, to find what she needed. They explained that the sawdust must come from a special young tree that she had to choose, and it had to be freshly cut. They would cut only one of the branches, the tree would grow as normal and the years of the tree would be parallel to the person that benefited from the sawdust, meaning that if the tree lived for a hundred years so would Moonlight.

'We will come for you before dawn. Tonight, you must rest, a hard day awaits you tomorrow.' They wished her goodnight and left. Esperanza was alone.

She looked around and noticed that what the cabin lacked in size it made up for in comfort. There was a small table covered with food, a comfortable bed and a little bathroom. She bathed, dined and went to bed. As she rested she whispered. Moonlight, can you hear me? Are you well? I am with the lumberjacks, they will help me get the sawdust tomorrow.'

'I am fine, thank you. You should get some rest, we will speak again tomorrow.'

The following morning, Esperanza woke early, made herself some breakfast, gathered her things and was ready to leave. When she opened the cabin door to her surprise and delight, Rose and Mary greeted her. The lumberjacks were also present. One of them approached her, extended his hand and asked Esperanza if she was ready to leave.

'Let's go.'

They quickly left the village behind and entered the forest. It was still dark, although day had already broken, but the sun was not high enough to cast its light between the trees.

The company walked in single file, Esperanza positioned herself in the middle. She was talking to a lumberjane, named Axe, who explained that in their society men and women took part in all the activities. Whether it be chopping down trees, building cabins, making a meal or taking care of the young and old. Esperanza, who was totally captivated by the peaceful humility shown by these beautiful people was not aware of the time it took them to reach their destination.

Two hours later they reached the spot they were heading to, a vast opening in the forest, full of young trees. During the trek, Esperanza had been keeping an eye on the twins, they were up to their normal tree climbing antics, just ahead of the group. Bob the head lumber-jack was the first to speak.

'Here you are Esperanza. Choose your tree.' Esperanza looked around, there were thousands of them. She called for Rose and Mary who in their usual urgency, appeared immediately by her side.

'There are too many, I do not know where to begin, can you help me.'

'Sure!' replied the squirrels. 'Follow us.'

The two squirrels were dodging in and out and up and down the trees, this time at a slower pace, so Esperanza could keep up. Then suddenly they stopped and stood perfectly still. When Esperanza reached them, they had their tails wrapped around the trunk of a young pine tree and were gesturing with their paws this one.

Esperanza called out to Bob, 'This is the tree.'

'Good choice, this one will live for many, many years. Where will you keep the sawdust?' asked Bob.

Esperanza reached for the jar. He sized it up and asked her to hold it under the spot and asked Axe if she would like to do the honours. She did not cut off the entire branch, but she cut precisely where she knew she would obtain enough dust to fill the jar, which was quickly filled to the brim. Esperanza screwed on the top and placed it carefully back in her bag. She embraced the young tree and thanked it for the dust.

As she walked away she shouted, 'thank you tree, thank you very much.'

A light gust of wind gently moved its branches, as if it was bowing in acknowledgement.

The company split up, most of them went off to their daily activities, Bob and Axe decided to walk with them a short way. Esperanza asked them why all of the young trees were in the middle of the forest and why the trees seemed to get taller and older as they advanced to the edge of the forest.

Axe explained, 'Many of the trees are over a hundred years old and were planted by our great, great grandparents. The oldest ones are on the outside, the trees then are younger as you reach the middle. As you follow the trees inward, you are following the work of each generation, the new generation is responsible for the new trees. Just where we made the cut, in a hundred years from now, the trees will be setup totally opposite to now, the older ones will be the young trees we just left behind, the young ones will be on the outside.'

'Each generation is responsible for our future and the well-being of the forest. We take great pride in our inheritance,' Bob added.

They all walked on together a while longer and then decided it was time for them to go back. Bob was the first to embrace Esperanza, then she was hugged by Axe, to whom she held on to a little longer.

'If ever I had a sister, I would like her to be just like you.'

'The feeling is mutual.'

'Thank you, thank you all.'

'Take care,' replied the lumberjack. 'We wish you well. You are very brave. The squirrels will take you to the crystal mountain, we will not keep you any longer. Goodbye'.

'Good bye and thank you once again.'

The rest of the walk through the Whistle-blowing woods was uneventful and just like the journey into the trees. Rose and Mary were climbing trees and switching sides every now and then, Esperanza walking steadily in the direction of the squirrels, dipping her hands in her bag for the occasional snack. The squirrels covered her ears when the wind got stronger. After many left and right turns, jumping over, going under and walking around some fallen tree trunks, they arrived at a point where the path branched into three. North, east and west, they all indicated a route to the mountain. Rose said that they should go west, Mary wanted to go east, Esperanza was confused. While the sisters were arguing their case, Esperanza held the blue stone and realised that the best way was north. She could see the path ahead and the mountain in the distance.

'North,' she said and started to walk in that direction soon followed by the sisters until they finally arrived at the foot of the mountain.

Rose and Mary were mounted on her shoulders, wrapping their tails around her neck like a scarf, creating a warm and cozy sensation. In spite of their hyperactivity she had become very fond of them. She stroked their tails and thanked them both. The sisters bid her farewell and were off; Esperanza once again was on her own.

THE CRYSTAL MOUNTAIN

The Crystal Mountain looked like any other mountain. It was very high with snow covering its peaks, like a big white wig, which ran down freely to its 'shoulders'. The pine trees, in an effort to cover the mountain completely, had only made it half way up whilst at the foot of the mountain lay a vast green valley, but there seemed to be nothing crystalline about it.

'Moonlight are you there?' whispered Esperanza. 'I have the gold and sawdust and I am standing at the bottom of the Crystal Mountain. I do not see anything special about it and I surely can't see any crystals.'

'As you ascend things will become clearer, find Glitter, she will help you.'

Esperanza began her ascent. It was midday, the air was thinner but warmer. She could hear birds chirping and caught sight of a few as they flew over her path. She could also hear the rustle of leaves as nervous rabbits and other inhabitants of the mountain would scuttle away as she approached on the path. She held the blue stone time after time, to see if she could catch a glimpse of the alicorn, but Glitter was nowhere to be seen.

What she did catch sight of was an owl sitting quite close to where she was. Esperanza decided she would ask for help. At the bottom of the tree she looked up and saw that he was asleep.

'Mr Owl,' she called. 'Please wake up, Mr Owl.' Then she shouted, 'Wake Up!'

'No need to shout,' said the Owl. 'I'm not deaf.'

'My name is Esperanza, I want to help Moonlight and I need to find Glitter. Do you know where she is?'

'It is always the same with you youngsters. "I want, I need, can I get." Always demanding and expecting instant results.'

'You don't understand,' pleaded Esperanza. 'This is not for me, it is for Moonlight. She needs help and I'm running out of time. I need to find Glitter, but she is nowhere to be seen. Do you know where she is? How can I get to her?'

'Calm down and sit down'.

'I don't have time to sit down. How can I calm down at a time like this? Thanks, Mr Owl. Just go back to sleep!' Esperanza started to walk away.

'Listen to the owl,' whispered Moonlight.

Esperanza returned to the bird and sat down.

'Now listen child. No one can see or find Glitter because she is never in the same place. You have to look for her in a different way. She can be seen and found everywhere on this mountain. So, close your eyes, relax and hope that when you reopen them, you will see her.'

Esperanza did as she was told, she closed her eyes, crossed her arms while holding on to the green stone and tried to relax. Once she was calm she opened her eyes and looked around. She saw nothing at first, so she closed her eyes once more. She opened her mind and her heart and that is when she could see the alicorn reflected in the trees, the branches, the leaves, the plants. Now it was clear to her that Glitter was indeed everywhere, she smiled and called out, 'Glitter I can see you, I found you.' The alicorn stood right in front of her.

She was completely snowy white, tall, strong and delicate. She had a long tail, a bushy mane, strong wings and the deepest, kindest grey eyes Esperanza had ever seen. She was beautiful. Esperanza hugged her neck, then climbed on her back. They did not need to say a word, the bond was so strong, they both knew what was expected from each other. They trotted up the mountain in perfect harmony like two beings with one soul. Esperanza felt totally at ease for the first time in her life, so she relaxed and enjoyed the ride. Her trust in this lovely creature was total and unquestionable.

Esperanza would ask the occasional question or make an occasional comment, Glitter would always respond with her calm, soft reassuring voice. When they reached the summit, Esperanza dismounted. 'Now what?'

'Can you see that little cave?' replied the alicorn. 'You have to go inside and look for a diamond that is about the size of your hand. When you find it, take it and throw it against the wall, it will turn into dust. Fill your jar and make sure to collect the remaining dust and fill the hole that was left in the wall where you found the diamond. I will be here when you return.'

Esperanza did not question Glitter's instructions. She held on to the white stone, made herself small and walked into the cave.

Once inside, she put on the helmet that Top gave her and turned on the light. The cave was a lot bigger than she had expected.

As she turned her head to look around, she could see the walls reflecting the light from her helmet which lit up the entire cave. The cave was deep and spacious and had five tunnels that formed a semicircle around the back wall. She entered the first one, but this one led to a dead end. The second one was similar to the first, the third seemed to be much longer and she felt that it was more promising than the others, but then she realised that the path circled around and led her back where she had started. She sat in the middle of the cave to calm down and regain her composure.

'Moonlight, can you hear me?'

There was no answer. She blamed the enclosure and decided to focus on the tunnels once more. She entered the fourth and felt that she was descending. At the bottom she was in a smaller cave that had a tunnel on the opposite side, she entered and noticed that she was now ascending. At the summit she exited and found herself back in the original cave. She screamed, 'What is going on? This place is so frustrating!'

She sat down once more, crossed her arms, held her necklace and closed her eyes. She even turned the light from her helmet off in order to focus. When she switched the light back on, nothing had changed. She was sitting in the same place, facing the same problem. Her necklace failed again and again. Frustration and anger combined began to get the better of her as she held the green stone and looked at the fifth and last tunnel.

Speaking to herself, she concluded that it was pointless coming all this way and getting this far to leave the last stone unturned. She thought about Moonlight and the frail state she must be in. She also reflected on all of those who had helped and encouraged her: Mr Top, the moles, Justin, Martha, Jill, the beavers, a salmon, Rose and Mary, Bob, Axe, the owl and Glitter.

'Last one, let's do this!' she exclaimed as she entered.

The last tunnel was different from the others, it had turns, first to the left, then to the right, another right and finally to the left. At the end of this last turn she found the cave growing much higher and saw a tunnel in the middle of the wall. She had to jump, hang on and pull herself up to get into this one. Then she crawled and entered a bigger cave. She could not see much, not because it was dark, on the contrary the walls reflected the light from her helmet and sent it back to her. So, she closed her eyes and switched off the light.

When she reopened them, she could see diamonds glinting all over the wall in front of her. She focused on one, walked straight to it, plucked it from the wall and switched the helmet light back on. All the diamonds disappeared except the one that was in her hand, she threw it against the wall and it turned into dust. The dust fell across the cave floor like light snow and covered everything, even her shoes. She took the empty jar from her bag and filled it to the brim, she screwed the lid back on and placed it carefully once more back in its place. Then she collected the remaining dust and placed it back in the hole and walked away. Just before she left the cave she switched off the light and saw that the diamond she had picked had fully restored. Puzzled she took the jar out the bag and could see that it was still full.

'Thank you diamonds,' she said and left. Glitter was waiting for her outside.

'I have all the three dusts, I need to get back to Moonlight.' Esperanza looked up at the sky. 'It is getting dark! The full moon is rising! I won't be able to get there on time. Glitter, what can I do? I have failed. It took me two and a half days to get this far, it will take me at least two days to get back. There is no way I can make it.' She started to cry.

'What would you need to get back in time?' asked Glitter.

'I would have to fly but I can't'.

'I know, but I can. Climb on my back and hold on to your green stone.'

She did as she was told. Glitter asked her if she was ready, then she extended her wings and they were off.

Esperanza for the first time had a birds-eye view of the countryside she had ventured through. It was hard for her to believe that she had covered so much ground. She could see the Crystal Mountain as they left, then she recognised the Whistle-blowing woods, next she saw the Blue River and knew that they were almost there. As they began to fly over the forest where her journey began, she held the blue stone and could see where Moonlight was lying.

'Left, Glitter, she's to the left, now to the right, she's down there, Glitter, she's down there.' They landed, Esperanza jumped off the alicorn's back and ran where the fairy lay. She was under the same mushroom. She looked so frail and her eyes were closed.

THE DUST

Esperanza took the sawdust jar from her bag and sprinkled it evenly over the mushroom. Then she gently picked the lifeless fairy up and placed her on the sawdust, face up, she extended her wings and stepped back. She opened the other jars and mixed the diamond and gold dust together. She sprinkled the dust evenly and carefully over Moonlight's body and wings, then she looked up to the moon and realised that a cloud was blocking the light.

'No!' She screamed. 'No!' She looked in despair at Glitter.

'Hold on to the green stone and don't give up,' said the alicorn while flapping her wings and flying directly to the cloud. Esperanza was crying while she watched Glitter fly away with Moonlight lying motionless on the mushroom.

Glitter flapped her wings frantically and pierced a hole in the cloud. The light got through and shone directly on Moonlight. Esperanza watched in total awe, as the light began to travel through Moonlight's body and then across her wings. It was like new blood running through her veins. The fairy sat up, stretched both her arms and wings, then she stood up and fluttered them.

'Yes! Yes! Yes!' Exclaimed Esperanza. 'You are well. Your wings have healed. Thank you Glitter, thank you so much!'

'No,' said Moonlight and Glitter together. 'Thank you, Esperanza.'

None of them could contain their happiness as they hugged, laughed and cried all at the same time. They had achieved what they set out to do and Moonlight's wings were healed. Their adventure had come to an end and it was time to say goodbye. But the bond between these three amazing beings would last forever.

'Now we must leave you. Whenever you need us, we will be here. All you have to do is call.'

Glitter was the first to leave, but not before she got a final hug. Moonlight stayed a little longer, she was sitting on Esperanza's knee.

'Let me look at you, you are so beautiful,' said Esperanza.

Moonlight was a reflection of the colours of the moon. She was different shades of grey. Her hair was long, with shades of black, grey and silver and almost reached her waist. Her eyes were dark grey which got lighter as they reached the centre. Her expression was profoundly gentle. Her wings were a translucent white, with dark grey veins and a full moon right in the middle, as if it were a tattoo.

'I love you Esperanza, I will never forget you'. She stood up and extended her wings, Esperanza could see the moon reflected in the middle of them.

'I love you Moonlight.'

'Goodbye Esperanza.'

'Goodbye Moonlight.'

'Goodbye, Esperanza.'

Esperanza was back in her secret place, and someone was calling her name. She looked up and took her mother's hand. Her mother hugged her tightly.

'Where have you been? I have been looking for you all over the place. What a lovely necklace, did you make it?'

'No mum, it was a gift from Moonlight'.

WILLWOOD

Lightning Source UK Ltd.
Milton Keynes UK
UKHW010808290720
367359UK00003B/955